TOTALLY SPACED!

TERENCE BLACKER

Ms Wiz
TOTALLY SPACED!

Illustrated by
TONY ROSS

ANDERSEN PRESS
LONDON

First published in Great Britain in 2008 by
ANDERSEN PRESS LIMITED
20 Vauxhall Bridge Road
London SW1V 2SA
www.andersenpress.co.uk

2 3 4 5 6 7 8 9 10

Ms Wiz Banned! first published in 1990 by Piccadilly Press Limited

British Library Cataloguing in Publication Data available.

ISBN 978 184 270 702 9

Printed and bound in Great Britain by Clays Ltd, Elcograf S.p.A.

To
Lily Holbrook

Ms Wiz

Ms Wiz

Ms Wiz

AND THE DOG
FROM OUTER SPACE

CHAPTER ONE
PSYCHO PUPPY

Tilly Davis looked into her worm farm and sighed. There was no doubt about it, she thought to herself. Worms were not the greatest of pets.

With her finger, she gently turned the earth which she had gathered from the park and put into a plastic box to provide a home for her worms. Slither, the biggest worm, seemed to be asleep. So was Twisty, his friend. A smaller worm with a mark on its body, whom Tilly called Scar, moved slowly across the surface of the earth.

"Scar moved, Mum," Tilly called out.

Tilly's mother bustled into the room, brushing her hair, putting on her watch and talking all at the same time.

"We're both going to be late," she said. "If I tell my boss that I missed the train because Scar the pet worm had decided to move a bit, I don't think she'll be very impressed."

Tilly covered the three worms with earth. "Don't you listen to her, Scar," she whispered. "She loves you really. What was that?" She leaned forward and seemed to listen to what the worm was saying. "Scar says you work too hard, Mum. He says you should chill out like he does."

Mrs Davis stopped brushing her hair and looked at her daughter. "Maybe it's time to let those worms go," she said more gently. "They aren't really meant to be pets, are they?"

Tilly nodded. "I suppose they've had their adventure in the world of humans," she said, standing up. "I'll take them back to the park later today."

"Well done, love."

"And then I'll get some more worms."

Mrs Davis put her hand on Tilly's shoulder. "What about having a proper pet?" she asked. "A hamster perhaps. Or a lovely little guinea pig."

"I don't believe in keeping animals in a cage," said Tilly. "It's like putting them in prison."

"And we happen to live in a small flat on the fourth floor which is much too small for a cat," said her mother.

"What about a dog?" Tilly asked.

Mrs Davis winced. "They take a lot of time, you know, what with walks and vets and, I don't know . . . fleas and things. I'm a very busy woman and you're at school."

Tilly sighed and picked up the worm farm. "So," she said sadly. "Worms it is."

Mrs Davis glanced at her watch. "On your way, then. Jack and Podge will be waiting for you downstairs."

Tilly kissed her mother at the front door to their flat. Then, holding the plastic box in front of her, she made her way down the stone steps.

As she reached the landing below theirs, a door opened to the sound of snarling and snapping and two large dogs, tugging at their leads, emerged, followed by a big lumpy teenager who was struggling to control them.

"Hi, Nutter! Hi, Psycho!"

Tilly crouched down in front of the dogs. Seeing her, they began to wag their tails and whimper. Both of them licked her face – it was like going

through a very smelly car wash. She glanced up at their owner, who was called Gary but who preferred to use his nickname. "Hi . . . Gob," she said.

"You want to watch out for them dogs," he said. "They're killers when they get nasty."

Tilly laughed. "They're just telling me that they want to be let off their leads and have a run in the park."

"Yeah, like they really talk to you," said Gary.

For the briefest of moments, Tilly thought about telling him that it was true, that she really could understand what dogs wanted – it was as if she could hear their voices in her head. But then she realised that Gary would just think that she was a bit odd.

"'Bye, dogs," she said, then turned to make her way down the last flight of steps onto the pavement where Jack and Podge, her friends from St Barnabas School, were waiting for her.

It was not a perfect day at school. During the morning, Class Five's teacher Mr Bailey talked to the class about how the world's climate was changing. Lizzie, who was very interested in the environment, said that if the icecaps started melting, polar bears might become extinct.

Jack said that would be really lame because polar bears were his favourite animals.

Caroline said she preferred hippopotamuses, especially when they yawned.

"I've got an aunt who's got two parrots," said Podge. "They fly round the sitting room and hang off the curtain and do poos on the mantelpiece."

"Excuse me, Class Five, this is not pet corner!" said Mr Bailey, rather more loudly than he intended. "We're talking about the future of Planet Earth not about pets and their toilet habits."

"Tilly's got worms," thought Jack. At least, he thought he had thought it but, when he noticed that everyone in the class was staring at Tilly, he realised that he must have said the words out loud.

"Worms, Tilly?" Mr Bailey seemed to have forgotten about Planet Earth for a moment. "Is this true?"

Tilly was blushing. "What's wrong with having worms?" she muttered.

"That's quite enough of this discussion," said the teacher. "Tilly, the nurse is coming in this afternoon. Please tell her that you've got worms. She'll give you some pills."

"Pills?" said Tilly. "Why would I need pills?"

Mr Bailey seemed oddly embarrassed. "Well, sometimes if you eat something, these little worms can start growing in your stomach," he said.

"Tilly's worms are in a box," said Podge. "They're her pets and their names are—"

"Podge!" warned Tilly.

There was a moment of unusual silence in class.

"Perhaps we could return to the subject of global warming," said Mr Bailey.

After school, Tilly, Jack and Podge went home together through the park. When they reached a flowerbed in the park, Tilly put the worm farm on the ground, then gently turned it over so that the earth and her three worms tipped out.

"Bye, Scar. Bye, Slither. Bye, Twisty. I'll miss you."

Podge put his hand over his mouth and squeaked, "And we'll miss you."

Jack nudged him in the ribs and frowned.

"Sorry, Till," said Podge. "See ya, Twisty and the others."

They wandered towards the park gate in silence. On their way, Tilly noticed a small, wooden shed. She was just about to say to Jack and Podge that she had never noticed it before when something small, hairy and black and white appeared at the door of the shed and hurtled towards them. From the way that it nipped Jack's ankle, then Podge's, it seemed to be some sort of angry little dog.

"Ow!" shouted Jack.

"It's attacking me!" said Podge, doing a scared little dance.

The dog stopped in front of Tilly. It sat down, wagging its tail, and looked at her expectantly, one ear up.

"Where's that puppy gone?"

A woman in a long brown overcoat,

holding a broom in her hands,
appeared at the door of the shed.

"It's psycho, that thing," Jack called
out. "You should keep it on a lead."

"She just chews through leads." The
woman walked towards them, then

looked down at the dog, which was still gazing up at Tilly. "She chews through everything."

"Yeah, like my leg," said Podge.

"Come here, Thingy," said the woman.

"Thingy?" Jack said to Podge. "Bit of a funny name for a dog, isn't it?

"Thingy!" the woman shouted. Then, sighing, she closed her eyes. A faint humming noise could be heard. As if being carried by invisible hands, the dog was lifted in the air and put down at the woman's feet.

As she leaned down to pat its head, Jack noticed that the park keeper was wearing black nail varnish.

"Ms Wiz?" he said. "Is that you?"

"Unless you know anyone else with a flying dog, it is," said Ms Wiz. "I said I go wherever magic is needed. The litter in this park is a disgrace."

"What's with the dog?" asked Podge.

"It was lost," said Ms Wiz casually. "I said I would give it a home."

From Ms Wiz's pocket emerged the head of Herbert, the magical rat. In each of his ears was stuffed some cotton. "Oh yes, and we don't worry about rats, do we? Because rats don't have feelings, do they? That horrible little Thingy is doing my head in."

For the first time, Tilly looked away from the dog towards Ms Wiz. "I know you're magic and all that but you really shouldn't call a dog 'it'," she said. "And Thingy's not a very nice name either."

Ms Wiz sighed. "I know it's not, but there was nothing on the list of names for the dogs of Paranormal Operatives that I particularly liked. I thought about Muttilda or Yapitha but they weren't quite her, somehow."

"She says her name is Ruby," said Tilly.

"Says?" Ms Wiz looked puzzled. "I know rats and cats can talk but Thingy – I mean, Ruby – has never said a word to me."

"Well, she's talking to me in my head," said Tilly. "She says she's called Ruby and she wants to find her mother."

Ms Wiz frowned slightly. "All right, I'll admit it. I'm impressed. I've seen all kinds of magic but I've never come across a psychic dog."

"Ruby says every dog can talk but that only a few humans can understand them. I happen to be one. And she really wants to know where her mum is."

"There is a bit of a problem there," said Ms Wiz. "Thingy – I mean, Ruby – has come from rather a long way away."

Herbert had pulled the cotton wool out of his ears. "There is absolutely no question of my returning to that horrible place," he said.

"Excuse me, Ms Wiz," said Tilly. "I thought you always said that you go wherever magic is needed. Just because it's a dog and not a human that needs help, you start making excuses."

"Yeah, but Ruby's mum could be anywhere in the world, right?" said Jack.

"Er, yes," said Ms Wiz quickly. "Almost right."

"And the last time she did a

travelling spell, Class Five got stuck on the sunny tropical island of Sombrero," said Podge.

"And Class Four were turned into pigeons," said Jack.

"Almost right?" asked Tilly. "Why did you say that, Ms Wiz?"

"It's just a little thing," said Ms Wiz. "But in order to find Ruby's mother, we would have to cross the universe to a distant planet. There's just a possibility we might take a wrong turning and end up completely lost in space."

"Yeah, don't you just hate it when that happens?" said Jack.

"Poor Ruby," said Tilly. "She'll never ever see her mummy again."

Ms Wiz seemed to be thinking. "Oh, all right," she said suddenly. "Let's all go into space for a while."

There was a moment of unenthusiastic silence in the park.

It was Podge who spoke first. "The problem is, I've got quite an important appointment. It's with some baked beans on toast back at my place."

"I've really got to do my homework," said Jack. "There's this really important geography project."

Herbert the rat wriggled out of Ms Wiz's pocket and down the leg of her trousers. "You can count me out, old girl," he said. "I do get so frightfully travel-sick."

"So it looks like just you and me then," said Ms Wiz to Tilly. "You hold on to one of Ruby's ears and I'll get the other."

"Are you going to freeze time while you step into another dimension?" Jack asked. "Otherwise Tilly's mum will be worried."

Podge groaned. "Why does time always stand still when it's time for my tea?" he said.

"There's no need for time to stand still," said Ms Wiz. "We'll be back soon enough." She closed her eyes and soon, all around them, could be heard a low humming noise. Gradually she and Tilly and Ruby faded from view.

Jack shrugged. "There's no talking to that Ms Wiz once she decides something."

"Well, at least I don't have to wait for my tea," said Podge.

"I think you do," said Jack, taking out his mobile. "We'd better call Mrs Davis and tell her that her daughter's in outer space looking for a dog."

From ground level, there was a small, polite cough. It was Herbert the rat.

"Ahem, I think you chaps may have forgotten something," he said. "All I'll be requiring is a nice warm armpit to sleep in and the occasional chocolate biscuit."

"Can't you look after yourself?" asked Jack. "Rats are famous for being able to survive anywhere."

"I think you might be mistaking me for an ordinary rat," said Herbert. "Now, be good lads and just pick me up."

Podge reached down for him and, before he could object, Herbert had wriggled between the buttons of his shirt.

"Aagh, it tickles,"

said Podge, writhing about a bit.

"Mmm." A muffled voice came from inside Podge's shirt as Herbert snuggled down. "Nice armpit."

CHAPTER TWO
ONE WEIRD PLANET

There are normally certain problems in travelling through space. You have to wear a spacesuit and helmet because there is no oxygen to breathe. You float about a bit because there is no gravity to keep you in your seat. If you go really fast, you can actually go back in time. In space, someone can pretty quickly become their own grandparent.

Fortunately for Tilly, magical space travel was different. It was simply a question of flying through the infinite blackness of the universe while holding on to a dog's ear and chatting as you go. As she, Ms Wiz and Ruby passed Mars, Ms Wiz was talking about her first pet, which had been a baby dinosaur.

"A dinosaur?" said Tilly. "You
know, I had no idea that you were
quite that old."

Ms Wiz smiled modestly. "I must
say that I really don't look too bad
for someone who has been knocking

around since the beginning of time. You know what the secret is, Tilly? A sensible diet, lots of exercise and at least three spells every day."

Tilly gazed across the universe. "I've always wondered what it was like during the Ice Age," she said.

"Brrr." Ms Wiz gave a little shiver. "Don't even talk about it. But let me tell you about my pet dinosaur…"

And so, as they flew past Mars, Jupiter and Pluto, Ms Wiz and Tilly chatted about pets until they reached the planet where Ruby had once been born. The journey took a little over twenty minutes.

As they entered the atmosphere of the planet, the sky around them changed from black to a pinkish grey and then to a bright gold. As the three of them landed gently on some grass,

Tilly realised that the gold came from a warm and friendly sun above their heads.

She looked around her. There were fields, trees, the sound of birds singing. Ruby was so excited that she galloped crazily in circles, yapping with joy.

Ms Wiz looked around her and smiled. "I've always thought it was rather a nice place. It's called Planet Grrr."

"It's just like the countryside on earth," said Tilly. "Look" – she pointed to a hillside nearby – "I think I can see houses."

"That would be Grrrtown, the only town on Planet Grrr. It's where all the Grrrians live."

"Funny name, Planet Grrr," said Tilly. "Is there any reason it's called that?"

"Yes," said Ms Wiz. "As it happens, there is."

On the other side of the universe, Tilly's mother was panicking.

"Let me just get this right," she said when Jack telephoned her. "You're telling me that you met up with an old friend called Ms Wiz in the park, that she has magic powers and a dog from outer space and that she's now gone off to a distant planet with Tilly and the dog."

"That's about it," said Jack. "I'm sure everything will be fine. After all, Ms Wiz is a grown-up – sort of, anyway."

From Mrs Davis's handbag, came the sound of her mobile's ringtone.

"I've got a text," she said. "It might be her."

"Er, Mrs Davis. She's in outer—"

"Bye."

Mrs Davis scrabbled in her bag for the mobile phone, then opened the text. It was from Tilly. She sighed with relief, then read what Tilly had written.

"gne in2 spce wth ms wiz. Bck sn. Txxxx."

Breathing deeply, Tilly's mother closed her mobile. "The important thing is not to panic," she murmured. "It's only . . . space, after all." She picked up the phone and dialled 999. "Hello, police," she said in a wobbly voice. "I'd like to report a missing person."

"So that's the reason it's called Planet Grrr," Ms Wiz was saying as they sat on a hill overlooking Grrrtown. "It's because the place is entirely run by dogs. Except on this planet they prefer to be called Grrrians."

"Weird," said Tilly. "And I can't believe that I can still text my mum from here."

"You couldn't in the old days," said Ms Wiz. "You had to use carrier pigeons. Now, thanks to modern magic, it's all much easier."

Tilly was wondering how exactly there could be carrier pigeons in space when suddenly she noticed some movement in the town. "There's a human over there!" she said. "So it's not just dogs."

"There are humans," said Ms Wiz carefully. "But they're not quite the same as us."

"They look the same," said Tilly.

"The humans here are actually pets,"

said Ms Wiz. "The Grrrians keep
them for fun and for doing tasks. On
Planet Grrr, humans are like horses
for humans back on Earth." She stood
up. "Perhaps we should take a closer
look."

Under the gentle sun of Planet
Grrr, Ms Wiz and Tilly walked slowly
towards the town. As they approached,
Tilly noticed that in front of each of the

little houses were beautiful wooden kennels.

In one street, the humans were making a new kennel for the dogs. Strangest of all, the humans were dressed exactly the same in a light beige tracksuit. At a park nearby, a group of humans were running around and playing, watched by three dogs who seemed to be talking among themselves.

"This is one strange planet," said Tilly.

"Yes, it is rather different," Ms Wiz agreed. "Look at the playground."

Tilly gasped. "It's for dogs!" she said. "There are balls everywhere and bones on strings that they can jump for. There's a toy cat that runs up trees. That's so sweet."

Ruby walked ahead of them and,

when Tilly called her, the dog ignored her.

"On Planet Grrr, humans follow dogs, not the other way around," said Ms Wiz, as she reached under a nearby bush and took out a small suitcase. When she opened it, there were two beige tracksuits. "Slip it on," she said. "From now on, we're Ruby's pets."

In their new beige pet uniforms, Ms Wiz and Tilly followed Ruby. When they reached the first house, Tilly noticed two humans in the back yard. They paced up and down the fence, saying, when they passed each other:

"Nice day."

"Nice day."

"Mustn't grumble."

"Takes all sorts."

Tilly shook her head. "It's like they can only do small talk – no real conversation," she said in a low voice.

"On Grrr, the humans just make friendly noises to each other," said Ms Wiz. "All the thinking is done by dogs."

Hearing them talk, Ruby turned and barked at them to stay closer.

"It's a nice place to visit, Planet Grrr," Tilly murmured under her breath. "But I don't think I'd want to live here."

CHAPTER THREE
WALKIES

"Jack Beddows and Peter Harris, also known as 'Podge'."

Sitting in an office at St Barnabas School, PC Boote made a careful note in his notebook. He glanced at the two boys sitting opposite him. They looked like troublemakers, he thought, but since they were the only witnesses to the disappearance of Tilly Davis, he had to take a statement from them. He wished he was out in a police car, chasing thieves with the light flashing and the siren going, like other policemen.

"All right, boys," he said. "Tell me in your own words what happened."

Jack and Podge took turns to tell the story of what happened in the park, as the policeman noted it down.

"Went to the park," he murmured as he wrote. "Buried some worms . . . Saw a small dog . . . Noticed the park keeper . . . Turned out to be Ms Wiz." At this point, PC Boote groaned to

himself. Whenever that Wiz woman was involved, trouble was never far away. "Decided to look for the dog's mother . . . Discovered it came from another planet . . . Tilly held its ears . . . Disappeared into outer space."

Slowly, PC Boote put his pencil back in his top pocket. "You should be aware, Jack and Peter, that wasting police time is a very serious offence – even if you are a bloomin' kid. You could end up in court."

"But they did disappear into space," Jack protested.

"Yeah, and I'm a Dutchman," said the policeman.

"Hm. The Dutch will be pleased." The voice – thin, posh and slightly muffled – came from the direction of Podge's armpit.

"What was that you just said?" PC Boote sat forward in his chair.

"Er, nothing," said Podge. "It's just that my armpit makes some funny noises now and then. It's a medical condition."

"Medical . . . condition." Because he couldn't think of anything to say, the policeman noted down the words. "Right. I have one last question. How did you know that the dog was missing its mother?"

Before either of them could answer, Herbert spoke from the direction of Peter's armpit. "Maybe it was feeling a little rough. Get it? Ruff! Ruff! Like a dog?" He chortled wheezily. "Sometimes I think I should be on the stage."

"Right, that's it." The policeman sprang to his feet. "I'm reporting you both for . . . inappropriateness. If I discover that Tilly Davis is not in space – which, frankly, I doubt very much – you both could end up in court."

Without another word, PC Boote stormed out of the room, walked quickly across the playground, jumped into his car and drove off with the tyres squealing.

"Oh dear." Herbert poked his head through the front of Podge's shirt. "Was it something I said?"

On Planet Grrr, things weren't going to plan either. Ruby lay with her chin resting on her paws in the kennel that had been found for her. Ms Wiz and Tilly were locked up with a few other humans in a house nearby.

Tilly had tried to talk to the humans but, although they seemed to understand, they would smile blankly and say something really boring, like "Turned out nice again" or "Takes all sorts, doesn't it?" or (a particular favourite) "Well, as long as you've got your health."

After a while Tilly gave up trying to talk to them. "The humans round here aren't exactly great at conversation," she murmured to Ms Wiz.

"They're pets," said Ms Wiz. "Their Grrrian owners don't like them to think too much."

Through the barred window, they noticed that Ruby was trotting towards the house. As she opened the door, the human pets began running about and jumping up and down in an excited way. Ruby barked once and the humans sat down, looking sorry for themselves.

She glanced towards Ms Wiz and Tilly.

"What's she saying to us?" asked Ms Wiz.

"Walkies," said Tilly.

Ms Wiz shook her head. "I really can't get used to being a pet," she said.

They followed Ruby out of the door and waited as she locked it behind her with her teeth.

Then she looked up at Tilly. When she had finished, Tilly turned to Ms Wiz.

"Ruby has been told that her mother isn't here," she said. "There's a rumour that she has been captured by the enemy."

"Enemy? Who could be an enemy of the Grrrians?"

Tilly frowned. "Cats," she said. "Ruby's mum has been captured by cats."

CHAPTER FOUR
A HISTORIC MOMENT
FOR RATKIND

Mr Harris, Podge's father, prided himself on being respectable. "I may not be rich and I may not be handsome," he used to say to Mrs Harris, "but at least I'm a respectable man. Isn't that right, Mother?"

"It certainly is," Mrs Harris used to say. "Respectability is your middle name."

So when his front doorbell rang and there, standing on his doorstep, was a policeman, Mr Harris assumed there had been a mistake. "Wrong house, young man," he said, making to close the door. "We're a law-abiding family here."

"You are the father of Peter Harris,

also known as 'Podge'?" said PC Boote in the deep, grown-up voice which he sometimes practised in front of the mirror when he was at home.

"I am," said Mr Harris.

"Then we need to have a little chat," said PC Boote.

The Harris family – Mr and Mrs Harris and, squeezed between them, their only son Podge sat on the sofa waiting

for PC Boote to find the right page in his notebook.

"I have made some very careful notes," he muttered. "It's just a question of finding them among the other crimes I'm working on."

"Crimes?" Mr Harris spoke sharply. "I'll not have talk of crimes in this house. Respectability's my middle name."

"Here we are." Smiling with relief, PC Boote smoothed down the page of his notebook. "I am currently investigating a very unusual case. Tilly Davis, young Peter's classmate from St Barnabas, has disappeared – allegedly to the other end of the universe."

"Other end of the universe?" said Mr Harris. "I've never heard such piffle—"

PC Boote held up a hand, as if he

was directing traffic. "Now we know that there has been text communication between Tilly and her mother. Mrs Davis asked Tilly where she was and received the reply—" The policeman checked his notebook. "'*Plnt Grrr*'." At this point in time, we do not precisely know what or where Plnt Grrr is."

"Plnt could be 'Planet'," suggested Podge.

PC Boote looked at him coldly, then smiled at his father. "We're not stupid down at the police station, Mr Harris. We know that nobody can text from the other end of the universe. It's way out of range. Unfortunately your boy and his friend Jack have gone along with this ridiculous story."

"But it's true," said Podge.

"And in addition," said the policeman, "your boy made some

extremely rude comments from the direction of his armpit."

"Odd?" said Mr Harris.

"Armpit?" said Mrs Harris.

Podge was just wondering how to explain what happened when Herbert the rat, who was under his shirt, made the decision for him.

"Can't *think* what the silly man's talking about," he said in a loud voice.

"There!" With a shaking hand, PC Boote pointed at Podge's armpit. "He's doing it again!"

"How on earth d'you do that, Peter?" asked Mrs Harris.

"It's a sort of magic thing," said Podge.

"Aha!" PC Boote leapt to his feet. "Now you're in trouble, young man." He thumbed through his notebook and took a piece of paper which he waved triumphantly. "This is an ASBO – an Anti-Social Behaviour Order. Normally ASBOs are to stop kids painting graffiti or vandalising property or frightening people. But this one's different." He glanced at the sheet in his hand. "It bans Ms Wiz, alias Dolores Wisdom, alias Diamante Wisporino, alias Dr Wisdom, alias Miss Wisbrowicz, from magic, spells or any paranormal—"

As the policeman was speaking, a long, loud and very rude noise came from Podge's armpit.

"Magic . . . spells . . ." PC Boote's normally pale face had gone quite red. "You're in breach of the ASBO. I'll take you down to the station, I will."

It was at that moment that there were signs of movement at the front of Podge's shirt. Herbert squeezed himself out and sat on Podge's lap.

Mrs Harris gave a little scream. "It's a rat!" she gasped.

"Calm down, young lady," said Herbert.

"A talking rat," said Mrs Harris, but then gave a little smile. "Did he say 'young lady'?"

"I am indeed a *talking* rat." Herbert gave a little bow in the direction of Mrs Harris. "It was not this charming young man who was doing the magic, but *moi*." He gave a little bow. "Herbert, the enchanted – the

enchanting – rat, at your service."

"Herbert, this is my mum," said Podge.

"Your mother? Impossible. She's much too young and much too . . . slim."

"Oh!" Mrs Harris seemed to be blushing. "He's quite charming for a rat, isn't he?"

"I may be a rat, madam, but I can appreciate a beautiful woman when I see one," said Herbert.

"Do you—" Mrs Harris looked down, smiling shyly. "Do you really think I'm beautiful?"

Mr Harris pointed an accusing finger at Herbert. "Is that rodent flirting with my wife?" he asked angrily.

"That's just the way he is, Dad," Podge said quickly. "He likes to be polite."

PC Boote loomed over Herbert. "Do you belong to Ms Wiz?" he asked.

Herbert gave a little laugh. "If anything, she belongs to me. Frankly, I'm the brains of the outfit."

"In that case," said PC Boote, "I have no choice but to arrest you for committing magic in a public place."

Herbert held out his paws in front of him.

"Handcuff me then, officer," he said in a tragic voice.

"Take me to the cells. I shall be a martyr to magic. 'Tis a far, far better thing that I do—"

"Shut it, rat," said PC Boote. "Save your speeches for the judge." He turned to Mr Harris. "Would you happen to have some kind of box so that I can take the accused into custody?" he asked.

"We certainly do, officer. The sooner that rat's off the premises, the happier I'll be."

"I thought he was rather nice," said Mrs Harris weakly. "Lovely old-fashioned manners."

"Why couldn't you just keep your mouth shut for a change, Herbert?" Podge muttered to Herbert.

"I shall not be silenced," said Herbert. "There are times when even a rodent has to stand up for his rights. This is a historic moment for ratkind."

Podge shook his head. "Earth to Ms

Wiz," he murmured. "You're needed back here – urgently."

Crawling through the undergrowth on Planet Grrr behind Ruby the dog, Ms Wiz was thinking she would quite like to be back on earth, too. "Dogs in charge, cat terrorists, humans as pets," she whispered to Tilly. "Aren't you glad you don't live here?"

Ruby looked over her shoulder, baring her teeth slightly.

"She's telling us to be quiet," said Tilly. "We're getting near the cats' camp."

They stopped. Across a small valley, there was a small wood. In the low branches of the trees of the wood was an extraordinary sight. There were hundreds of cats of all colours and sizes. In a clearing beyond them could

be seen five dogs. As Tilly and Ms
Wiz watched, one dog tried to escape.
The cats let it run for a while, then
surrounded it.

"They're playing with the dog as if
it's a mouse," Tilly whispered.

Ruby whined.

"Perhaps Ruby could divert the cats'
attention," said Tilly. "Then we could

sneak round the back and— "

But Ms Wiz had stood up. "I think it's time to stop being a pet."

Ruby growled.

"She's telling you to sit," said Tilly.

But Ms Wiz was walking down the slope of the valley, then up the other side. As she approached, the cats turned towards her, ears back, hissing.

"Nice puss-pussies," said Ms Wiz. "Kitty kitty."

The cats crouched down, their hackles rising.

"Oh, suit

yourself," said Ms Wiz. There was a low humming noise and suddenly, in the place of the cats, there were hundreds of mice.

"They've just learned an important lesson," said Ms Wiz as the mice scurried for cover. "It doesn't pay to mess with humans – especially paranormal ones."

A streak of black and white dashed past her into the wood. Soon Ruby and a dog that looked just like her were tumbling over one another yelping with excitement.

Moments later, Tilly arrived. "I think Ruby may have found her mum," she said.

CHAPTER FIVE
BIG PLACE, THE UNIVERSE

In Grrrtown, a group of dogs surrounded Ms Wiz and Tilly. There was growling, yapping, snapping and snarling. Now and then one of the larger dogs would bare its teeth in the general direction of Ms Wiz.

"Well, I must say, that's not very grateful." Ms Wiz was trying not to look scared. She looked down to their feet where Ruby and her mother, whose name turned out to be Grendel, were cowering.

Tilly was following the conversation of the angry dogs that surrounded them. "Some of the Grrrians are saying it was great that the cat terrorists have all been turned into mice and the hostages rescued but most of them are angry that it was a human pet who did it. And they're worried you might turn them into mice, too."

"They're right to be worried," said Ms Wiz. "I'm very tempted indeed."

As she spoke, a dangerous silence descended on the pack of dogs.

"Ah." Ms Wiz smiled as bravely as she could manage. "It looks as if the Woof Parliament has just managed to make up its mind."

Tilly didn't laugh. "Ms Wiz," she said urgently. "I think it's time for us to go."

The dogs moved closer, their eyes glinting, a low growl in their throats. Then, distantly, another noise – a sort of hum – could be heard.

"Very slowly," said Ms Wiz quietly, "lean down and hold Ruby's ears. I'll hold on to Grendel. Hang on." She closed her eyes. "I've just got to turn the mice back into cats."

When she looked again, the dogs were crouching, ready to pounce. The growling grew louder.

"Now, Ms Wiz!" screamed Tilly. "Now!"

Back on earth, Tilly's mother was just arriving at the police station, followed by Podge and Jack. In spite of the texts that she had received from Tilly, she was becoming more and more worried about her daughter being lost in space. Travelling across the universe accompanied by a Paranormal Operative and a dog just wasn't natural.

She pushed through the door of the police station and strode up to the desk where PC Boote was standing. "I believe you have arrested a rat," she said. "I need to talk to it."

PC Boote squared his shoulders. "I am not at liberty to divulge who is in custody at this police station, human or rat," he said.

"But we know he's here, constable," said Podge in his sweetest, most polite voice. "I saw you take him away in a shoe box."

PC Boote looked bored. "I repeat, I am not at liberty to—"

With a sudden movement, Mrs Davis reached out and grabbed the front of PC Boote's uniform. As she brought her face close to his she seemed to lift him off the ground. When she spoke, it was quietly and through gritted teeth.

"My daughter is missing, believed

lost in space. The rat knows where she is. We are going to talk to the rat right . . . now. It's really a very simple matter."

"B-b-but there's an ASBO." The policeman's eyes glanced left and right, looking for help. But he was on his own.

Mrs Davis tightened her grip. "D'you want me to get seriously angry?" she asked.

"Put me down," PC Boote said hoarsely. "And I'll take you to the rat."

Herbert was locked up in a cage on a table in a brightly lit room. He was not happy. As soon as Tilly's mum, Jack

and Podge followed PC Boote through the door, he started complaining.

"I am not used to this treatment," he said in weak, tired voice. "It's uncomfortable. I can't sleep. There's no one to talk to. And the toilet facilities are frankly unforgivable."

Mrs Davis shook her head in amazement. "You were right, Podge. It really does talk," she said.

"That will be 'he', if you don't mind, madam," said Herbert.

"*He* would be well advised not to talk any more," said PC Boote. "A talking rat counts as magic in my book and right now magic is against the law."

"But if humans are allowed to speak, why can't I?" asked Herbert. "This is rattism, pure and simple."

Mrs Davis pulled up a chair and sat by the table so that she was at the same level as the cage. "Mr Herbert, we would like very much to know where Ms Wiz has gone with my daughter. All we know is that she's somewhere in the universe."

"Hmmm." Herbert scratched the side of his nose. "Big place, the universe."

"Herbert," said Podge sharply. "This isn't a joke."

Suddenly the light bulb in the room flickered, then faded. For a few seconds, there was darkness. Then slowly, with a distant hum which grew louder and louder, the light returned.

The room was crowded now with two extra people. They were crouched on the floor and each seemed to be holding the ears of a dog.

"Ms Wiz!" said Jack.

"Tilly!" said Mrs Davis.

"Mum!"

For a moment, there was confusion in the police station. Tilly ran into her mother's arms. The dogs barked. Ms

Wiz explained to Jack and Podge what had happened. PC Boote tried to keep order.

In his cage, Herbert closed his eyes wearily. "The same old Ms Wiz," he murmured. "She just has to be the centre of attention."

PC Boote moved purposefully towards Ms Wiz. From the top pocket of his uniform, he took out his notebook. "Ms Wiz, I am arresting you for committing magic in breach of your ASBO."

"Magic?" Ms Wiz looked puzzled. "Who on earth is Asbo?"

"As a specific example of the heretofore mentioned illegal magic, I have noted the following: being in possession of a talking rat—"

"Booooooring," Herbert sang out.

"—disappearing to the other side

of the universe," PC Boote continued. "And appearing out of thin air in a police station without having first reported at the front desk."

Ms Wiz was smiling dangerously. "Is that all?" she said quietly. "I can do much better spells than that." A humming noise filled the room. PC Boote looked around, suddenly confused.

"What was I going to say?" He frowned to himself. "Why am I carrying this notebook? Why am I in a uniform? What am I doing here?"

"Your memory is now entirely blank," said Ms Wiz.

"But who am I?" said PC Boote. "I don't even know my name."

"Now." Ms Wiz ignored the policeman. "Let's get things sorted out. Herbert, you poor old thing." She opened the cage and held out her hand.

Murmuring, "You have simply no idea what I've been through," Herbert wriggled into Ms Wiz's sleeve and up her arm, from where his muffled voice could be heard complaining. "She sugars off to the other side of the universe and does she give a thought for me? Not a chance. I'm just a rat, I'll be all right. It's just me me me with that Ms Wiz . . ."

"What are these dogs doing here?" asked Tilly's mother.

Ms Wiz groaned. "Why did I agree to bring them both back to Earth? I can't possibly look after two dogs."

At her feet, Ruby whined. Tilly listened for a moment, then whispered in her mother's ear. Mrs Davis glanced down at Ruby, who put her head on

one side and cocked her ear as if
waiting for a reply.

"Ms Wiz," said Tilly. "Ruby asked
me if she can come and live with us
and my mum, I think, has just agreed."

"And I would keep Grendel."
Ms Wiz smiled with relief. "It's perfect.
That puppy was exhausting me. They
can meet in the park now and then."

She knelt down beside Ruby.

"You stay here," she whispered. "I'll

see you soon." She held onto Grendel's ear and closed her eyes. A faint humming noise could be heard.

"Wait!" shouted Podge. "What about—?" He nodded in the direction of PC Boote, who was still looking about like a man lost in a maze.

Ms Wiz stood in front of him and looked into his eyes. "You are a community policeman," she said quietly. "Your name is Gavin Boote."

The policeman blinked twice, then sighed sadly. "Do I have to be?" he asked.

But Ms Wiz and Grendel were fading from view. Very faintly, a voice could be heard.

"See you in the park, Tilly."

There was a single bark of farewell from Grendel, and then silence.

* * *

On Planet Grrr, two human pets were talking.

"Nice day," said one.

"Mustn't grumble," said the other. "As long as you've got your health."

"Remember that human pet who came to visit – the one who rescued the hostages from the cats?" said the first.

"Yeah."

"Well, I've been thinking . . ."

Ms Wiz
BANNED!

CHAPTER ONE
A FRIEND IN NEED
IS A FRIEND INDEED

Just because you can do a few magic spells, and fly, and turn people into animals now and then, it doesn't make life any easier. Sometimes being a Paranormal Operative can be really hard work.

"Yes," said Ms Wiz, putting the telephone on to boil. "Being magical is no bowl of cherries, that's for sure."

She was in her flat and had a tough day ahead of her, doing her homework, learning new spells and revising the old ones.

Then there was the housework. Ms Wiz looked at the list of things to do which she had pasted on a notice-board in her kitchen. It read:

1. Tell the vacuum cleaner to do the bedroom.
2. Put a washing and ironing spell on a dirty pile of clothes.
3. Speak roughly to the duster about the book shelves which haven't been touched for weeks.

"Flats don't clean themselves, you know," she said to Herbert, the magic rat, who was asleep in the corner.

"You can help me by cleaning out
your cage right now."

Herbert twitched his nose and went
back to sleep.

"Just a quick cup of tea," Ms Wiz
said to herself. "Then I'll get on with
those spells." She glanced at the
telephone and sighed. It was true
what people said – a watched
telephone never boils. Just then the
teapot rang.

"Hullo," said Ms Wiz, picking up the lid.

"Er, you won't remember me," said a man's voice from the teapot. "But I'm a school inspector. We met once at St Barnabas School."

Ms Wiz smiled. The last time she had seen the School Inspector, he had been running across the play-ground without his trousers on after Herbert the rat had run up his left leg.

"Of course I remember you," she said.

"We have a bit of a crisis here," said the School Inspector. "I wouldn't have called you but you're my last hope. We need your help."

"Tell me about the crisis," said Ms Wiz.

"Well," said the School Inspector, "it all began at yesterday's morning assembly . . ."

*

84

It had all begun at yesterday's morning assembly.

The highlight of assembly at St Barnabas was when the head teacher Mr Gilbert spoke about his Thought for the Day. This lasted for five (or, if it was a particularly big Thought, for ten) minutes and could be about any important subject.

One day the Thought might be "A Friend in Need is a Friend Indeed." Or "Great Oaks from Little Acorns Grow." Or "Neighbours, Everybody Needs Good Neighbours."

The children of Class Five liked Mr Gilbert's Thought for the Day. It gave Katrina the chance to finish the homework she should have done the previous evening. Her friend Podge used those few minutes to eat a couple of chocolate biscuits he had brought in his pocket. And Podge's friend Jack, who always went to bed too late, could catch up on some sleep.

But yesterday, the day of the crisis, Mr Gilbert's Thought had been most unusual.

"I think," he said, "I think I'm going to be sick."

Because so many of the children were busy doing their homework, or eating, or sleeping, no one paid much attention. But then Mr Gilbert sat down heavily on one of several empty chairs in the front row.

At that moment, Miss Peters leapt to her feet and said quickly, "Now, children, until Mr Gilbert feels better, we'll sing our favourite song, 'Lord of the Dance'." She sat down at the piano and, with a brave smile, began to sing "Dance, dance, wherever you may be."

"He won't be doing much dancing," whispered Katrina to

Podge, as the head teacher tottered down the aisle and out of the door. "Who's going to run the school now? Miss Gomaz, Mrs Hicks and Mr Williams are all ill too."

"Perhaps we'll all be sent home," said Podge when he had finished his biscuit.

"... Otherwise they'll all have to be sent home," the School Inspector said to Ms Wiz the next day. "We need someone to run the school for a week. We're desperate."

"You want me to be the head of St Barnabas?" Ms Wiz could hardly believe her ears.

"And we need other teachers too," said the School Inspector.

"Leave it to me," said Ms Wiz. "Your crisis is over."

"And, er, Ms Wiz." The School

Inspector sounded embarrassed.

"May I make one small request?"

"Of course."

"Go easy on the magic, all right?"

Ms Wiz sighed. Why *was* it that people were so nervous about a few spells these days?

"Trust me," she said.

At the next morning's assembly, the children of St Barnabas noticed that there was a stranger sitting in the Head Teacher's chair. She wore a dark suit, a black gown and had a funny square hat on her head.

"She doesn't look much fun," Caroline whispered to Katrina.

"Come back Mr Gilbert, all is forgiven," said Katrina.

The woman stood up and said quietly, "Good morning, children. My name is Miss Wyzbrovicz. I'm

Mr Gilbert's replacement. I'd like to introduce you to my two assistants who are here to help me this week."

From the front row, a small, neat woman in glasses and an older, grey-haired man stepped forward and stood on each side of her.

The new head teacher took off her hat, and shook her head, allowing long dark hair to fall on her shoulders. Then she started clicking her fingers. "One, two, three, four," she said.

To the astonishment of everyone in assembly, the woman's two assistants started clapping their hands in time.

"What on earth?" muttered Jack who, for the first time in living memory, was awake during assembly.

Suddenly the head teacher began to talk – or rather to sing.

"Morning, everybody, get into that beat,
Listen to me, children, and tap those feet."

"I don't believe it," said Katrina.

"The head teacher's doing a song," said Podge.

"It's morning assembly and your feet's a-tappin'

As you hear your new head teacher a-rappin'."

Now the grey-haired man joined in, singing,

"My name's Mr Warlock, now listen to me,

I'm here to teach ya some geographee."

"A rap song?" said Jack, his jaw sagging. "At St Barnabas morning assembly?"

The other teacher stepped forward.

*"I'm Miss N Chanter but don't be
   afraid
I'll show you how magic potions are
   made."*

"Magic potions!" Caroline smiled. "That must be it. When things get this strange, there can only be one person behind it."

"Of course," said Podge. "Look at the black nail varnish on the head teacher's hands."

Soon the whole of Class Five were clapping in time to the song.

The head teacher smiled, pointed the fingers of both hands at the children and sang,

*"So, kids, I'm here to teach you the biz
You know me, my name's—"*

"Ms Wiz!" shouted everyone in Class Five.

Outside the School Hall, the School Inspector listened. He had a busy day ahead, but was just calling by to see that the new head teacher was settling in all right. From the sounds coming from assembly, she seemed to getting on well, even if it was a bit noisy.

"Phew," he said, glancing at his watch. "At least there's no magic around."

CHAPTER TWO
TRAVEL BROADENS THE MIND

No magic?

The children of Class Five who clustered around Ms Wiz after assembly were shocked by the news she brought them.

"What about Herbert the rat?" asked Caroline.

"And flying around the classroom on your vacuum cleaner?" asked Katrina.

"And turning teachers into warthogs?" asked Jack.

Ms Wiz held up her hands for silence.

"The School Inspector has invited me to St Barnabas on condition that there's no magic," she said.

The children groaned.

"Why?" asked Katrina.

"Because spells make grown-ups nervous, that's why," said Ms Wiz, putting on her square hat. "So I'm going to be a serious head teacher."

"Who's in charge of Class Five this week?" asked Caroline. "Mr Williams is off sick."

"I've given you Mr Warlock," said Ms Wiz. "I think you'll find him very interesting, but this is his first teaching job. Can I depend on you to be nice to him?"

"You can depend on us," said Jack. "We're Class Five."

"That's what worries me," said Ms Wiz.

"Is it true that you're a wizard, sir?"

"Jack!" hissed Caroline. "Remember what Ms Wiz said."

Mr Warlock stood at the door of the

classroom and stared in amazement at Class Five.

"Excuse me for asking," Jack continued, ignoring Caroline. "It's just that I've got a book at home called *Witches, Warlocks and Other Weird Creatures*."

Katrina put up her hand. "And the other new teacher's called Miss N Chanter," she said.

"Nicola Chanter, yes," said Mr Warlock.

"N Chanter. That means that she *enchants*, doesn't it?"

Mr Warlock took off his glasses, laid them on the desk and looked at Class Five very seriously.

"I don't know what you're talking about," he said. "I'm just as normal as any other teacher."

"Which isn't very normal," murmured Jack.

"All right," said the new teacher. "Answer your names, please." He read

out the register. There was only one person missing and that was Carl, the youngest boy in the class.

"Carl's always late," said Lizzie. "He probably thinks it's a Saturday."

The teacher frowned and made a note of Carl's name.

"Now today we're going to do some geography," he said, unrolling a map of the world that he had brought with him and pinning it on to the blackboard. "Who likes geography?"

There was silence from Class Five.

"Learning map signs," muttered Podge. "Discovering the difference between an isthmus and a peninsula. That's really interesting, isn't it?"

Mr Warlock looked surprised.

"Well," he said, reaching into his briefcase, "I think you'll like it after today."

He laid a box on his desk and took out three darts.

"Who knows the capital city of Norway?" he asked.

Caroline put up her hand.

"Oslo," she said.

Mr Warlock gave her a dart.

"And the highest mountain in the world?"

Jack put up his hand.

"Mount Everest," he said.

Mr Warlock gave him a dart.

"And who can give me the name of a major European city where there are no pedestrian crossings?"

There was silence. Mr Warlock smiled and put up his hand.

"Venice," he said. "Because all the streets are canals." He gave himself a dart. "Well done, Mr Warlock," he said.

"This is a *normal* teacher?" muttered Jack under his breath.

"Now, the two children with darts should come to the front of the class and throw them at the map," said Mr Warlock.

Caroline went to the front and threw her dart. Then Jack did the same. The teacher was about to throw his dart when Katrina asked, "What's this got to do with geography, sir?"

Mr Warlock looked surprised.

"Didn't I tell you?" he said. "I'm

taking you on a field trip to the most interesting place one of the darts lands on."

Caroline looked at where her dart had stuck in the map.

"Mine's in Milton Keynes," she said. "And Jack's is in the middle of the Atlantic Ocean."

"Oh dear, that's not very interesting," said Mr Warlock. He threw his dart, which made an odd humming noise as it flew through the air.

"Where did it land, Caroline?" he asked.

Caroline looked closely at the map.

"On a small island called Sombrero," she said. "It's in the Caribbean Ocean."

Mr Warlock smiled. "That's more like it," he said.

"I still don't see what's wrong with

Milton Keynes," muttered Podge, but no one was listening.

It wasn't that Carl meant to be late for everything. It was just that things were always happening to him that didn't happen to other people.

On this particular morning, for example, a cat followed him down the street. Since he was going towards a main road, he had to take the cat back to where he had first seen it. But then the cat followed him again. He took it back. On his third trip, carrying the cat back, its owner came out of the house and thought Carl was trying to steal it. It took quite a long time to explain the problem, by which time Carl was late for school yet again.

Nervously, he knocked on the head teacher's door.

"Come in," said a voice from inside.

Carl was surprised to find a woman sitting at Mr Gilbert's desk. She was playing chess with a rat.

"I was looking for Mr Gilbert," he said.

The woman smiled. "I'm head teacher this week," she said. "You can call me Ms Wiz."

"Ms Wiz!" said Carl, who had only

come to St Barnabas that term. "I've heard about you. You're the person who appears whenever a bit of magic's needed, aren't you?"

"That's right," said Ms Wiz. "Now what's the problem?"

Carl took some time to explain why he was late for school.

"I went to my classroom but no one seems to be there," he said.

"Really?" Ms Wiz looked concerned.

"All I could find was a notice on the blackboard," Carl said. "It read, 'GONE ON A FIELD TRIP TO THE SUNNY TROPICAL ISLAND OF SOMBRERO – BACK SOON!' What could that mean?"

"I think," said Ms Wiz, who had gone quite pale, "that it means I'm in dead trouble."

CHAPTER THREE
ASK NO QUESTIONS, HEAR NO LIES

"I *knew* it," said Ms Wiz, as she hurried across the playground with Carl running behind her. "I knew those two would start casting spells as soon as my back was turned."

"Which two?" Carl asked.

"Mr Warlock and Miss N Chanter," said Ms Wiz. "They're both Paranormal Operatives. Magic is as natural to them as flying."

As *flying*? Carl frowned. "But why didn't you just tell them to be normal?" he asked. "After all, you are head teacher. They're supposed to be able to boss people around."

Ms Wiz groaned. "I'm just not the bossing kind, I suppose," she muttered.

When they arrived at Class Five's empty room, Ms Wiz went straight to the map on the blackboard and pulled out three darts that were sticking into it.

"Oh no," she said. "Warlock's been using his magic darts again – and he's left them behind. Heaven knows how he'll get Class Five back here again."

Carl was looking at Class Five's lockers. "They won't be here for lunch anyway," he said. "They've taken their lunchboxes."

Ms Wiz sighed. "We'd better go and see Class Four," she said. "I don't trust Miss Chanter either."

As they entered the classroom next door, Carl couldn't help noticing that there was an unusual number of pet rabbits hopping about the room.

"Wow," he said. "I never knew Class Four kept rabbits."

Miss Chanter smiled and looked around the room.

"The class don't keep rabbits," she explained. "They *are* rabbits. If they can't spell properly, I'm turning them into—"

"No no *no!*" shouted Ms Wiz suddenly. "No magic, no spells, no rabbits, no potions, no broomsticks! I've already lost Class Five to a sunny tropical island. Turn these rabbits back into children immediately."

Grumbling, Miss N Chanter uttered a spell. Before Carl's astonished eyes, the rabbits became children once more.

"That's better," said Ms Wiz. "From now on, Miss Chanter, it's the three Rs for Class Four. Reading, writing and—"

"Rabbiting about?" suggested Jamie, a small red-haired boy sitting at the back of the class.

"No," said Ms Wiz. "Responsibility. I expect you all to be responsible while I try to get your friends in Class Five back from the other side of the world."

"Well, really," said Miss N Chanter, after Ms Wiz and Carl had left the room. "She used to be such fun before she was head teacher."

"It's always the same," said Jamie. "Class Five get the excitement and we get the telling off."

"Yeah." The rest of the class joined in. "It's really unfair, Miss."

The teacher scratched her head thoughtfully. "Perhaps I could take you on a trip around town," she said.

"We've seen the town," said Mary, who was sitting beside Jamie. "We live here."

"Yes," said Miss N Chanter. "But have you seen it from the sky?"

*

Ms Wiz had the nastiest surprise
imaginable when she returned
to the office with Carl. The School
Inspector was waiting for her.

"Good morning to you, Ms Wiz,"
he smiled. "I was just passing by and
I thought I'd look in to see how you
were getting on."

"Er, quite well, thank you," said Ms
Wiz nervously. "Everything's going
swimmingly."

"And who's our young friend
here?" the School Inspector asked,
nodding in Carl's direction.

"He's in Class Five with Mr
Warlock," said Ms Wiz.

"They've gone on a field trip," said
Carl quickly.

The School Inspector nodded.
"Where to?" he asked.

Ms Wiz had turned quite pale. Then
she straightened her back and said,
"I cannot tell a lie. Mr Warlock

appears to have taken them to Sombrero."

"And where precisely is Sombrero?"

There was another silence, during which the clock in Mr Gilbert's office could be heard ticking.

"It's a small island in the Caribbean," said Ms Wiz weakly.

It was at this moment that Carl saw something out of the office window which attracted his attention. Miss N Chanter was opening a door and a flock of pigeons was following her into the sunlight. One of them was the same colour red as Jamie's hair.

"Are you telling me that an entire class has disappeared to the other side of the world?" There was a faint hint of panic in the School Inspector's voice. "Am I to understand that there has been magic on these premises in spite of my specific instructions?"

Ms Wiz nodded miserably.

The School Inspector leapt to his feet.

"Right, that's it," he cried. "Rats up trouser legs are one thing – disappearing children are quite another. I'm calling the police and then I'm going to the Town Hall. I'll get you banned for life! Now, please pack your things and go. You will not be allowed back on the premises."

"But, sir," said Carl. "How are you going to get Class Five back if you ban Ms Wiz?"

The School Inspector looked at Carl as if he were about to swat him like a fly.

"There are such things as aeroplanes," he said nastily.

After he had left, Ms Wiz slumped into her chair.

"I should never have agreed to be a head teacher," she groaned. "Magic and a sense of responsibility don't seem to go together."

"Oh well," said Carl, anxious to cheer her up. "At least he didn't see the pigeons."

"Pigeons? Did you say pigeons?"

"They just walked out of Class Four's door and flew off," said Carl.

Ms Wiz had buried her face in her hands and was making an odd moaning sound.

"Let's just hope they're homing pigeons," said Carl.

The sun shone brightly on the lovely tropical island of Sombrero. The waves of the bright blue Caribbean lapped softly on the white sand and a gentle breeze carried the sound of calypso guitar across the beach. It was certainly the best field trip that Class Five had ever been on.

Katrina and Caroline sat under a palm tree, listening to a man playing a guitar, fanning themselves with their exercise books. Jack had found a skateboard ramp nearby and was showing the local children some tricks. Podge had cracked open a coconut and was using the top of his pen as a spoon. Lizzie was collecting seashells, and the rest of the class were paddling in the waves.

"Anyone got the time?" asked Mr

Warlock, sleepily sipping an orange drink through a straw. "We must remember to get back home before tea-time."

"Haven't you even got a watch?" said Lizzie, as she inspected a starfish.

"Must have left it at home in my case," said Mr Warlock. "It's probably with the magic darts."

"So how are we going to get home then?" asked Lizzie.

"That's just what I was wondering," yawned Mr Warlock sleepily. "I expect Ms Wiz knows the spell."

CHAPTER FOUR
LOOK BEFORE YOU LEAP

One of Mr Gilbert's favourite Thoughts for the Day was "When One Door Closes, Another One Opens." If Ms Wiz had been asked for her Thought this particular day, it might have been "When One Door Closes, The Ceiling Falls Down On Your Head." Or . . . "Just When You Think Things Can't Get Worse, They Do." Or . . . "Help, Get Me Out Of Here!"

Class Five had disappeared to the other side of the world.

Class Four had taken wing and were flying around in the clouds.

The School Inspector was reporting her to the police and was about to get her banned from the school.

"The important thing is not to panic," said Carl, as they sat in the head teacher's study, wondering what to do next.

"Yes, good, absolutely right," said Ms Wiz, panicking.

"If we can just get the two classes back by the end of the day," said Carl, "we can pretend that the School Inspector invented it all."

Ms Wiz sat up straight in her chair and looked at him sternly.

"I cannot tell a lie," she said.

"Of course not," said Carl. "Anyway, you're magic. I'm sure you can do it."

Ms Wiz sighed. "But I don't know the travelling spell," she said.

"Oh dear," said Carl gloomily.

"Of course, Miss N Chanter knows it but she's too busy being a pigeon to be much use."

"Oh dear, oh dear," said Carl even more gloomily.

Ms Wiz stood up suddenly, picked up her chair and walked towards the door.

"We'll just have to go and get help," she said. "Bring your chair to the playground, will you, Carl?"

"My *chair*?" Bewildered, Carl followed her out of the room, carrying his chair.

Moments later, amid a loud humming noise, Carl and Ms Wiz were hovering a few feet above the playground.

"Flying chairs!" Carl gasped. "Don't we need seat belts?"

"Of course not," smiled Ms Wiz. "This is magic."

The chairs rose high above the school, turned slowly towards the east and rose into the clouds.

"Where are we going?" Carl shouted above the sound of the wind whistling past his ears.

"Headquarters," said Ms Wiz.

Headquarters? Carl remembered Lizzie saying that she had seen Ms Wiz's home, an old car, when she had helped rescue Lizzie's cat from burglars, but no one had ever mentioned headquarters.

"Is it far?" he asked.

"Beyond Ongar," said Ms Wiz.

Beyond Ongar! Carl had never heard of Ongar, let alone a place beyond it.

Soon the chairs were descending rapidly through the clouds, coming to rest in a quiet back street in front of a tall office block with dark windows. By the entrance, there was a sign which read "PO HEADQUARTERS".

"Here we are," said Ms Wiz, jumping off her chair. "The headquarters of the Paranormal Operatives."

"I always thought PO stood for Post Office," said Carl.

"So do a lot of people," said Ms Wiz with a smile. "They keep sending their parcels here."

"That explains why the post is always late," Carl muttered as he followed Ms Wiz through some glass doors and into the building.

At first he thought that the office reception area was like any other. Then he noticed that all the people working there had black nail varnish. And that there was a sign on the wall which said "REMEMBER! WE ARE NOT WITCHES! WE ARE PARANORMAL OPERATIVES." And that a secretary nearby was reading a book called *Notions for Potions – Some Paranormal Recipes* while the keyboard beside her worked itself.

Ms Wiz walked up to the reception desk.

"I have urgent business with the travel department," she told the receptionist.

"Would that be time travel, space travel, inter-continental travel, inter-galactic travel, underwater travel, mind travel or holiday bookings?" the woman asked, filing one of her black fingernails.

"I need to get some children back from the other side of the world," said Ms Wiz.

"That'll be inter-continental travel," said the receptionist sleepily. "Mr Broom, our inter-continental travel executive, has gone for lunch in the Seychelles."

"Then get him back," said Ms Wiz sharply.

"I don't have the spell, do I?" said the woman.

"Who has got it?" asked Carl, thinking that at this rate they would never get Class Five back by the end of the day.

The woman looked at him coldly.

"Mr Broom," she said. "And he's gone for—"

"Enough!" Ms Wiz slammed the desk. "If you don't want to spend the rest of the day as a toad, you'll get him right now."

The woman shrugged. "Room 305 on the third floor," she said. "I'll see what I can do."

When Ms Wiz and Carl reached Room 305, they found a young man wearing a bathing suit and dark glasses sitting behind the desk.

"This had better be important," he said moodily. "I was just going for a swim in the sea when I was called back."

"It is," said Ms Wiz. "It's a case of missing children."

Mr Broom frowned as Ms Wiz explained the situation. Then he turned to a computer beside his desk and tapped some keys on the keyboard. Within seconds, a tropical scene appeared on the screen.

"There appears to be some sort of beach party going on," said Mr Broom. "Can you see any of your friends, young man?"

Carl moved nearer to the screen. "There's Podge at the barbecue," he said suddenly. "And Katrina's dancing by the radio. Mr Warlock seems to be asleep under a tree."

"Are you sure you want to get them back?" asked Mr Broom. "They seem to be having a very good time."

"Absolutely," said Ms Wiz. "All good things come to an end."

"Well, first of all you have to get the magic darts," said Mr Broom.

"But they're at St Barnabas," said Ms Wiz. "And I'm not allowed back."

Mr Broom shrugged. "Then you'll just have to find someone to work the spell for you," he said.

And suddenly Ms Wiz was smiling at Carl.

CHAPTER FIVE
SMALL IS BEAUTIFUL

There were times when Carl wished
that he wasn't late for everything,
and that afternoon, as he walked
through the gates of St Barnabas
carrying a pencil case, was one of
them. If it hadn't been for the cat
following him this morning, he would
be with Class Five now, enjoying the
sun and sand of Sombrero.

Instead he was the only person in
the world who could bring them back
and save Ms Wiz from getting into
more trouble. He was going to cast
a spell, like a real Paranormal
Operative. It was a bit dangerous, Ms
Wiz had said, but she trusted him.

As far as Carl could remember, this
was the first time that anyone had

ever trusted him with anything.

The School Inspector was pacing up and down inside the school gates like a watchdog.

"What are you doing, young man?" he asked suspiciously.

Carl held up the pencil case that Mr Broom at PO Headquarters had given him.

"I forgot my pencil case," he said. "I went home to fetch it."

The School Inspector did not look entirely convinced. "You haven't seen that Ms Wiz woman, have you?" he asked. "She seems to have vanished into thin air."

"That's because you banned her," said Carl.

"Hmm," said the School Inspector. "Just as long as she's not lurking about somewhere."

Inside the pencil case, Ms Wiz clung on to a fountain pen for dear life. She had agreed to help Carl with the travelling spell by making herself small enough to be smuggled into school.

From inside the case, she heard Carl telling the School Inspector that he had to fetch his books from Class Five's room so that he could work in the library. The pencil case shook as he ran across the playground.

Once again Ms Wiz gripped the fountain pen.

"The things I do for magic," she sighed.

As soon as they were in the classroom, Carl opened the case and carefully lifted Ms Wiz on to the desk.

"There's no time to lose," she said. "Grab the darts and I'll tell you the spell you've got to say."

"*I've* got to say?"

"I thought you wanted to see Sombrero," said Ms Wiz.

"I do, but—"

"Fine," smiled Ms Wiz. "You've got half an hour to travel across the world and bring your friends back. It's a piece of cake."

"What will you do while I'm away?" Carl asked.

"I suppose I'll have to hide in this case," said Ms Wiz. "The School

130

Inspector seems to be looking out for me."

"I won't be long," said Carl, holding the darts tightly in his hand. Repeating the words after Ms Wiz, he muttered the spell. Suddenly there was a humming noise and, for a few seconds, Carl felt like an arrow flying through the air, buffeted by the wind. He squeezed his eyes shut until the shaking stopped. Then he heard voices.

"Hey, it's Carl."

"What's he doing here?"

"Late as usual."

"Wake up, Carl. You're just in time for the limbo competition."

Slowly Carl opened his eyes. It was warm. The sunlight was dazzling. He could hear the distant sound of waves. And, all around him, were the children of Class Five.

"Phew," said Carl, dusting himself down. "I made it."

"Come and do the limbo," said Katrina. "You have to lean back and dance under this low pole. It's great."

Carl looked doubtful. "We haven't got much time before we have to get back," he said.

"Carl worrying about the time," Jack laughed. "I've heard everything now."

"All right," said Carl. "Someone go and wake up Mr Warlock. I'll have a

quick limbo and then we'll be on our way."

Back at St Barnabas, Ms Wiz sat in the darkness of Mr Broom's pencil case and thought about the past.

She remembered her adventures with the children of Class Five – the prizegiving when Mr Gilbert was turned into a sheep, the time when a

local hospital was invaded by white mice, the hunt for Lizzie's stolen cat, the day when Jack let loose ghosts and demons in a library, her adventures in a television set with Caroline and Little Musha.

"I've certainly been there whenever magic was needed," she said to herself. "But maybe it's time to move to another school. Or even to another country."

She paced up and down in the darkness. Carl had been gone almost ten minutes now. What if the spell had sent him to the wrong place? Or he couldn't remember how to get back? Or he had lost the magic darts? If something happened to her friends, she would never forgive herself.

But then Ms Wiz smiled. Outside the pencil case, she heard a distant hum which grew louder and louder. Suddenly the classroom was alive with the sound of children's voices.

"Wow," Podge was saying. "I've just had the weirdest dream. I thought I was on a tropical island."

"That was no dream," Carl said. Ms Wiz felt the pencil case being lifted, its top opened slowly. She looked up and saw familiar faces looking down at her. "That was Wizardry," Carl smiled.

Ms Wiz climbed out of the pencil case and stood on the desk. It was difficult behaving like a serious head teacher when you were only three inches tall, but she had to give it a try.

"Now where's Mr Warlock?" she asked.

"He wanted to go straight home," said Carl. "So I gave him the spell and the second dart."

"I think he was embarrassed at being unable to get us back," said Lizzie.

"Quite right too," said Ms Wiz. "Now, since I've been banned from the school, Carl is going to have to smuggle me out."

"What happens if the School Inspector asks where we've been?" asked Jack.

Ms Wiz straightened her back and looked at him sternly. "You should say, 'I cannot tell a—' "

"I think we should lie," said Carl firmly. "Just this once."

"All right," said Ms Wiz. "Say you went to a museum."

At that moment, there was a loud thudding noise on the roof of the classroom.

"That will be Class Four," smiled Ms Wiz. "Miss N Chanter's very punctual. Can they get down all right?"

"There's a ladder leading down from the roof," said Katrina.

"Good," said Ms Wiz, as a pigeon appeared at the window, hovered for a moment and then flew off. "Miss Chanter's off home." She glanced at a clock on the wall. "It's time for you all to go too. Your parents will be waiting for you."

"When will we see you again?" asked Podge.

"Well, right now I'm going to take a holiday," said Ms Wiz, reaching inside the pencil case and pulling out some bright yellow trousers. "I've even brought my holiday clothes."

"But you'll be back, won't you?" asked Caroline. "Whenever magic's needed?"

Ms Wiz paused as she climbed back into the case. "I hope so," she said with a smile, before closing the lid over her head.

Carl walked home slowly. Just once he looked inside the case. There, in the corner, was the tiny black dress of a head teacher.

Carefully putting it into his jacket pocket, Carl went over the strange, magical events of the day, wondering whether he would ever see his paranormal friend again. He smiled at the thought of her.

"Bye, Ms Wiz," he said quietly.